Mariah's Gift

Suellen Oliver Campbell

Copyright © 2017 by Suellen Oliver Campbell. 751612
Illustrated by Dennis Davide
Library of Congress Control Number: 2017911732

ISBN: Softcover   978-1-5434-4017-1
        Hardcover   978-1-5434-4018-8
        EBook   978-1-5434-4016-4

Print information available on the last page.

Rev. date: 07/28/2017

To order additional copies of this book, contact:
Xlibris
1-888-795-4274
www.Xlibris.com
Orders@Xlibris.com

Written with love for Barrett, Campbell, Eliot, Cora, and all of my Bridge Class children. May each one of you discover and embrace your own special Gift!

Out in the desert, at the foot of an old palo verde tree, Mother Coyote had made her den.

Mother Coyote had chosen the spot quite carefully. Her coyote instinct told her it was the perfect place for a home. The spreading branches of the palo verde tree provided shade for her den on hot summer days, and the golden sand absorbed the slanted rays of the afternoon sun making a warm bed on cool nights.

Nearby there was a high mound of large, misshapen desert rocks for climbing, and a small, sandy watering-hole within trotting distance of the den.

Towering above the desert floor there grew many magnificent saguaro cactus. Each cactus provided a safe habitat in which a variety of desert critters could call their home. Tiny elf owls had homes high up in the saguaro, and doves rested in nests they made on its arms. Families of jackrabbits made burrows at the feet of the saguaros, and in the Springtime busy gila woodpeckers made new holes in the cactus for their families. Hummingbirds drank the sweet nectar from its flowers and all manner of insects crawled up and down its spiny skin.

One warm day, the saguaro dwellers noticed there were to be new neighbors just across the sandy desert floor from them. They watched with interest as Mother Coyote began to dig under the palo verde tree.

It was hard work, and Mother coyote dug furiously at the foot of the old tree. Sand flew behind her as she used her paws to dig around the tree roots. Farther and farther down she dug until she was satisfied the den was deep enough for protection. It was there she had given birth to four lively coyote pups.

The coyote pups felt safe and protected when Mother Coyote snuggled close to them. Her soft fur was like a warm, fuzzy blanket when the pups cuddled next to her, and she was always on guard for any danger that might invade their home.

After keeping watch all night as her pups slept, Mother Coyote sniffed the early morning air and scanned the desert carefully for any sign of a predator. The dawning day was quiet and Mother Coyote began to close her tired eyes as the sun crept slowly over the desert floor toward the den.

Mother Coyote was napping when the first ray of sunlight made its way into the den and shone on the face of the littlest coyote. This one's name was Mariah.

Mariah was the smallest of the coyote family and she possessed a great curiousity about the desert world that lay outside the family den. Mariah had never been outside, but Mother Coyote had told her little family many wonderful stories about the desert world.

Mariah had a great desire to see the desert for herself. She had so many questions in her head: How wide were the spreading tree branches of the palo verde that shaded their den? How tall were the saguaros that housed so many desert creatures? How high was the pile of desert rocks? How cool was the water in the watering hole?

Mariah rolled over, sat up and looked at her mother who was sleeping peacefully. Her three brothers were also fast asleep. At that moment Mariah decided to leave the den for the first time in her young life.

She tiptoed softly across the sandy floor of the den. Under and over the roots of the palo verde tree, Mariah climbed up to the daylight and to the world outside.

The sunlight was bright and Mariah's green eyes sparkled when she saw her desert neighborhood for the first time. How exciting it was to behold the desert with all its wonders.

Mariah looked up and saw the spreading branches of the palo verde tree that shaded the den below. She looked out and gazed at the tall saguaros. Even farther away she could see the curious mound of rocks Mother Coyote had described to Mariah and her brothers.

Mariah was both amazed and fascinated. There was so much to see and experience that she set out right away to explore the neighborhood.

The sand was warm under her little paws and Mariah was excited about her desert adventure. She trotted a short distance until she reached the base of a very tall saguaro cactus. Looking up she could see it had many arms stretching above her head and beautiful blossoms on the very top.

Flitting around the blossoms was a tiny bird. It was quite busy drinking nectar from the flowers and, with great interest, Mariah watched it from below as it moved from flower to flower.

Mariah called out: "Hello, neighbor. What are you doing up there?"

The little bird stopped, glanced down at her, then quickly zoomed toward Mariah's head. It stopped in mid-air, hovered there, and chirped, "I am drinking my breakfast, and who are you? I have never before seen you in the neighborhood."

"My name's Mariah and I live under the palo verde tree with my family. This is the first time I am away from our den."

"It's nice to meet you, Mariah. My name is Hummer. I drop by this cactus for breakfast nearly every morning. Are you hungry? Would you care to join me for a sip of delicious nectar?"

"How nice of you," replied Mariah, "but I don't see how I can get up there."

"Well, first you have to flap your wings really fast and hover."

"Hover? What's that?" asked Mariah.

"Well, it's when you flap your wings so fast you can stop in midair and stay there without falling." said Hummer. "By hovering you can sip and sip as long as you want."

"Wow! That sounds difficult." said Mariah. "How did you learn to do that?"

"I did not learn how to do it, I just did it! It's my gift from the Loving Spirit of the Desert."

"A gift from the Loving Spirit?" asked Mariah.

"Yes, the Loving Spirit of the Desert gives each of the world's creatures a wonderful gift. It is what makes each of us unique and special."

"Do I have a special gift, too?"

"Of course you do. The Loving Sprit gives a special gift to everyone." said Hummer.

"I can't wait to try it out so I can drink nectar." said Mariah excitedly. "What do I do first?"

"You flap your wings and off you go. Simple as that," exclaimed Hummer.

Mariah tried, but she was a coyote not a hummingbird. She had legs instead of wings. Mariah jumped up into the air and fell down, over and over again. She flapped her legs as fast as she could, but she could not hover.

Finally, exhausted and out of breath, Mariah panted, "No matter how hard I try, Hummer, I cannot hover. I guess the Loving Spirit of the Desert did not give me a special gift after all."

"Nothing could be farther from the truth, Mariah. The Loving Sprit gives everyone a gift, but each creature's gift is different. My gift is to be able to hover, but your gift will be something special just for you. Before you were born the Loving Spirit knew you and chose your Gift. Now, it is up to you to discover what it is and how to use it."

"Thank you, Hummer, for your advice and for being my first friend," Mariah said. "I think I'd better be on my way now so I can discover my special gift. Have fun hovering and sipping nectar."

As Mariah trotted out farther out into the desert, Hummer shouted after her, "I'll be waiting to hear all about your gift!"

Mariah had not gone very far when she came upon a most curious creature. It had a hard shell on the outside of its body, mighty-looking pinchers, and a curved tail which it had arched over its back.

The creature was quickly moving back and forth and sideways.

Hello," said Mariah, "Who are you and what are you doing?"

The creature stopped and spoke in an excited voice. "My name is Serape and I am a scorpion. I am practicing my special gift."

Mariah said, "Oh, you were given a gift by the Loving Spirit of the Desert. Hummer told me everyone has been given a gift, but I don't know what mine is."

"Yes, everyone has received a gift from the Loving Spirit," answered Serape.

"My gift is to dance the Tinga-Cha-Linga. It requires much practice, but I think you could learn it if you try."

"I'd like to learn to dance the Tinga Cha-Linga." said Mariah. "How do I begin?"

"Well, first you hold your tail up high and then quickly walk forward four steps, stop, and quickly walk backward four steps," instructed Serape. "Now step to the right four steps, then step to the left four steps. Jump up and down four times, spin around and start all over again."

"Wow!" said Mariah. "I don't know if I can remember all that."

"Well, that's why you saw me dancing," said Serape. "It takes lots of practice to learn the Tinga-Cha-Linga."

With Serape as her teacher, Mariah tried to learn the Tinga-Cha-Linga. She tried, over and over, but Mariah's little coyote feet kept getting all tangled up.

"I don't think my gift is to dance the Tinga Cha Linga," said Mariah sadly.

"Maybe the Loving Spirit of the Desert forgot to give me a special gift."

"No, that is not possible!" exclaimed Serape. "The Loving Spirit gives every creature a special gift, Mariah. Keep searching and you will surely discover what your gift is."

And so Mariah said goodbye to Serape and continued to trot across the desert floor. Both Hummer and Serape had told her she had a special gift from the Loving Spirit. Mariah was now very determined to discover what the gift was that she had been given.

Before long, Mariah was suddenly passed by two speedy creatures. One had a long beak and tail with grey and black feathers, and the other had long ears and light-brown fur.

"Wow!" Mariah shouted, "You two are very fast runners! Who are you?"

Screeching to a stop, the creature with the feathers and long tail said, "I am Roadrunner. Who are you?"

"My name is Mariah and I am searching for my special gift from the Loving Spirit of the Desert. My new friends Hummer and Serape told me I have a gift, but I don't know what it is."

"Well, that's a coincidence." said the creature with light-brown fur. "I am Jackrabbit, and we are out practicing our special gift."

"Do you hover or dance the Tinga-Cha-Linga?" Mariah asked Roadrunner and Jackrabbit.

"No," said Roadrunner. "Those gifts were not given to us."

Mariah was concerned, "Were you sad when you realized you did not get the special gift to hover or dance?"

"Oh, no," answered Jackrabbit. "The Loving Spirit had other gifts for us that are more useful in the desert to a jackrabbit and a roadrunner."

Mariah was curious and asked in her soft voice, "What gifts did the Loving Spirit give you?"

Jackrabbit and Roadrunner jumped up and down and shouted excitedly at the same time, "We can run FAST!"

"That IS a useful gift for the desert." said Mariah. "You can catch food or run from predators with a gift like that."

"Yes! And we love to practice running. Want to race with us, Mariah? Maybe it is your gift too."

"Sure!" said Mariah, "I'll give it a try," and she got ready to run with Jackrabbit and Roadrunner.

"On your mark, get set, GO!" shouted Jackrabbit and off they all ran. The three new friends ran past the saguaros and palo verde trees, then around the towering rocks and the watering hole.

Jackrabbit and Roadrunner stayed out in front all the way, and when the race was over, Mariah came in last.

Her feet hurt and her tongue was hanging out.

"I don't think the Loving Spirit of the Desert gave me the gift of running fast," panted Mariah. "Maybe Hummer and Serape are wrong. Maybe the loving Spirit *did* forget to give me a special gift."

Mariah's little coyote eyes began to fill with tears.

Jackrabbit and Roadrunner came close and whispered softly in Mariah's ears, "Please don't be upset, Mariah. The Loving Spirit never forgets to give every creature their very own special gift. Be patient. Do not give up. You will discover it one day. You will!"

Mariah looked in the faces of her two friends and was convinced they were right. She was sure the Loving Spirit of the Desert would not forget even a creature as small as she. Mariah knew she did have a special gift, but it must be hidden deep inside of her, waiting to be revealed.

Mariah had been gone from her family all day, and so after saying goodbye to Jackrabbit and Roadrunner, Mariah began to slowly trot across the desert, back to her den under the palo verde tree. All the while she was thinking about her special gift from the Loving Spirit and wondering how soon she would discover it.

Back at the den it was getting late. Mother Coyote had been very worried about her littlest coyote and was anxiously waiting for Mariah to return.

The sun was beginning to set when she saw Mariah in the distance, trotting toward home. Mother Coyote hurried out to greet her daughter as the last rays of sunlight dipped below the horizon.

Mariah told her mother all about meeting her new desert friends, and that she had been searching all day for her special gift from the Loving Spirit of the Desert. She told her mother she had tried to hover, to dance the Tinga-Cha-Linga and to race across the desert floor. Sadly, the only thing Mariah had discovered was that *none* of these gifts were *her* special gift.

Mother Coyote nodded her head. "I understand that you want to search for your special gift, Mariah.

It is true what your friends say, that you have received a special gift from the Loving Spirit.

The Loving Spirit of the Desert does give each of the creatures their own particular gift, but as you have discovered, their gift may not be the same as yours."

Then Mother Coyote whispered quietly to little Mariah, "Climb to the highest place on the nearby mound of rocks. I am sure the Loving Spirit of the Desert has given you a special gift."

Mariah's feet were sore, and she was hungry and very tired from her long day, but she did as Mother Coyote told her. Mariah slowly padded over to the rock tower and began to climb as high as she could. She jumped from rock to rock looking for safe places to put her feet, to keep from falling.

Finally, Mariah reached the top. A full moon was rising in the sky above her and she could see the desert below, gleaming in its light. The shadows of the saquaros were spreading across the desert floor and the sweet aroma of their flowers filled the air.

When she stood atop the rocky mound, Mariah began to think about all the new friends she had met that day and the many special gifts that the Loving Spirit had given to each of them. Mariah felt happy thinking about what their friendships meant to her and the encouragement they gave while helping her search for her own special gift.

Mariah had tried and failed every time, but her friends had shown her kindness as she did her best to hover, dance and run. They could have made fun of her, but instead they helped her. Most importantly, Mariah's new friends told her that the Loving Spirit of the Desert would never have forgotten her.

While the moon rose higher in the darkening sky, Mariah's heart began to overflow with thankfulness for the wonderful day she had had in the desert. Suddenly, without even thinking, Mariah looked up to the heavens, opened her little coyote mouth and began to sing.

Mariah sang and she sang. Her song was carried by the night breeze across the desert sands and up into the starry sky.

For a long time that night, Mariah sang her song of thanks to the stars above and to the earth below. Mariah sang with joy in her heart while countless creatures of the desert paused and listened to her.

On that same moonlit evening across the desert floor, Hummer, Serape, Roadrunner and Jackrabbit also heard Mariah's beautiful song and they all happily agreed,

"Mariah has now discovered *her* very own special gift from the Loving Spirit."

And the Loving Spirit smiled.

The Loving Spirit has given each one of us a special gift, too. Have you discovered yours?

How to Dance the Tinga Cha-Linga

1. Take 4 steps forward (starting with your right foot)
2. Take 4 steps backward (starting with your right foot)
3. Take 4 side-steps to the right (starting with your right foot)
4. Take 4 side-steps to the left (starting with your left foot)
5. Jump and down 4 times
6. Spin around and start again

CPSIA information can be obtained at www.ICGtesting.com
Printed in the USA
LVIW01n1637161117
556555LV00011B/114